Popr and

'a/22

deleted

and th

Big Wave

For Marianne
SG

For Andrew with love x
LG

Reading Consultant: Prue Goodwin,
lecturer in education at the University of Reading

ORCHARD BOOKS
338 Euston Road, London NW1 3BH
Orchard Books Australia
Hachette Children's Books
Level 17/207 Kent Street, Sydney, NSW 2000
ISBN: 978 1 84362 398 4 (hardback)
ISBN: 978 1 84362 519 3 (paperback)
First published in hardback in Great Britain in 2007
First paperback publication in 2008
Poppy and Max characters © Lindsey Gardiner 2001
Text © Sally Grindley 2007
Illustrations © Lindsey Gardiner 2007

1 3 5 7 9 10 8 6 4 2 (hardback)
1 3 5 7 9 10 8 6 4 2 (paperback)
Printed in Hong Kong
Orchard Books is a division of Hachette Children's Books,
an Hachette Livre UK company
www.orchardbooks.co.uk

Poppy and Max and the Big Wave

Sally Grindley  Lindsey Gardiner

ORCHARD BOOKS

One morning a letter arrived for
Poppy and Max.
"Brilliant!" said Poppy. "I love
getting letters."

"My turn to open it," said Max.
He sniffed the envelope. "It smells
of seaweed."
Max pulled out the letter, looked it up
and down, and then gave it to Poppy.

Sniff
Sniff

"It's from our friend Tom," she cried.
"He wants us to go and visit him by
the sea."

"Yippee!" cried Max. "We can
chase crabs."

They packed a bag and went to
the station.
"My turn to sit by the window," said
Max when they got on the train.

"I can't wait to walk along the beach and watch the waves crashing on to the sand," said Poppy.

"I can't wait to chase crabs," said Max.

Tom met them when they got
off the train.

"I thought we could go surfing,"
said Tom.

"Brilliant," cried Poppy.

Max looked a bit nervous. "But I like
chasing crabs," he said.

"We can do that later," said Poppy.
"It's good to try new things."
They ran down to the beach.

"Look how big the waves are!"
cried Poppy.
"Perfect for surfing," said Tom.
"I am *not* going in there," said Max.

"There's no need to be scared, Max,"
said Poppy.
"I am not a dog who likes salty paws,
that's all," said Max crossly.

"Sit and watch us then," smiled Poppy,
"and afterwards we'll chase crabs."

Poppy and Tom walked to the edge
of the sea.
Max sat down grumpily to watch.

"Look at me," cried Poppy as she floated away on her surfboard.

"Look at me," yelled Tom as he stood up on his surfboard.

"It's brilliant, Max!" screamed Poppy.

"So is chasing crabs," muttered Max.

He looked along the beach.
He saw something scuttle across
the sand.

"It's a crab!" he cried. "Quick, Poppy!"
Poppy didn't hear him.

"I'm not waiting," said Max.
He dashed towards the crab.
It disappeared down a hole.
"Missed it," cried Max.

A tiny crab scuttled in front of him.
He pounced at it. It disappeared under
a rock.

"Missed again," cried Max. "Hurry up,
Poppy," he called. "You're missing all
the fun."

Poppy and Tom waved at him.
"Come on in, Max," they called.
"You're missing all the fun."

A crab popped up out of a hole and
scuttled towards the sea.
Max bounded after it.

He was just about to pounce on it
when a big wave swept over the top
of him. It lifted him off his feet.
"Whoooaaaa!" howled Max. "Put
me down!"
The wave rolled him over and over.

Fuck. you

Then his feet found something hard.
An arm held him round the waist.

"Hello, Max," said a voice. "I thought
you didn't like getting salty paws."

Max blinked the sea from his eyes
and found himself standing on
Tom's surfboard.

"Whoooaaaa! Put me down!" he
howled when it wobbled.
"I won't let you fall," laughed Tom.

"Brilliant, Max," called Poppy. "I'm glad you changed your mind."
She sailed past them, waving madly.

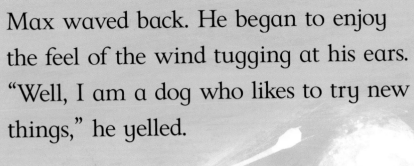

Max waved back. He began to enjoy
the feel of the wind tugging at his ears.
"Well, I am a dog who likes to try new
things," he yelled.

It was teatime when they walked back
up the beach.

"I'm sorry, Max, but it is getting too late to chase crabs now," said Poppy. "Never mind," said Max. "Chasing crabs is for pussycats, not adventurous dogs like me."

Poppy and Max

Sally Grindley
Illustrated by Lindsey Gardiner

Poppy and Max and the Lost Puppy	978 1 84362 394 6 £4.99
Poppy and Max and the Snow Dog	978 1 84362 404 2 £4.99
Poppy and Max and the Fashion Show	978 1 84362 393 9 £4.99
Poppy and Max and the Sore Paw	978 1 84362 405 9 £4.99
Poppy and Max and the River Picnic	978 1 84362 395 3 £4.99
Poppy and Max and the Noisy Night	978 1 84362 409 7 £4.99
Poppy and Max and the Big Wave	978 1 84362 519 3 £4.99
Poppy and Max and Too Many Muffins	978 1 84362 410 3 £4.99

Poppy and Max are available from all good bookshops,
or can be ordered direct from the publisher:
Orchard Books, PO BOX 29, Douglas IM99 1BQ
Credit card orders please telephone 01624 836000 or fax 01624 837033
or e-mail: bookshop@enterprise.net for details.

To order please quote title, author and ISBN and your full name and address.
Cheques and postal orders should be made payable to 'Bookpost plc'.
Postage and packing is FREE within the UK
(overseas customers should add £1.00 per book).

Prices and availability are subject to change.